A Charlie Brown Thanksgiving

LITTLE SIMON
An imprint of Simon & Schuster Children's Publishing Division
1230 Avenue of the Americas, New York, New York 10020
Copyright © 2002 by United Feature Syndicate, Inc. All rights reserved.
PEANUTS is a registered trademark of United Feature Syndicate, Inc.
All rights reserved, including the right of reproduction in whole or in part in any form.
LITTLE SIMON and colophon are registered trademarks of Simon & Schuster.
Manufactured in the United States of America
10 9 8 7 6 5 4 3 2
ISBN 0-689-85027-1

Adapted from the works of Charles M. Schulz

A Charlie Brown
Thanksgiving™

By Charles M. Schulz
Adapted by Justine and Ron Fontes
Art adapted by Tom Brannon
Based on the television special produced
by Lee Mendelson and Bill Melendez

LITTLE SIMON

New York   London   Toronto   Sydney   Singapore

On Thanksgiving Day, Charlie Brown stood sadly at his mailbox watching Snoopy walk off with a stack of mail—all for him!

Sally came up and asked, "What's the matter, big brother?"

"Nothing," Charlie Brown replied. "I was just checking the mailbox."

"What did you expect," Sally asked, "a turkey card?"

Charlie Brown sighed. "Holidays always depress me."
"I know what you mean," Sally said. "Why should I give thanks on Thanksgiving? What do I have to be thankful for?"

Linus walked up and asked, "What's all the commotion?"

"We've got another holiday to worry about," Charlie Brown grumbled. "Thanksgiving is here."

"I haven't even finished my Halloween candy," Sally wailed.

"Thanksgiving is important," Linus explained. "Our country was the first to make a national holiday to give thanks."

Sally looked at Linus and sighed and said, "Isn't he the cutest thing?"

When Charlie Brown and Sally went inside, the phone rang. It was Peppermint Patty.

"Listen, Chuck, I have a treat for you," she said. "My dad's been called out of town. He said I can join you for Thanksgiving."

Charlie Brown didn't know what to say. "Well . . . I . . ."

"I don't mind inviting myself because I know you kind of like me, Chuck," Peppermint Patty continued.

"Well . . . I . . ."

"Okay, it's a date," Peppermint Patty said. "See you soon, you sly devil."

"Oh, brother," Charlie Brown said. "Peppermint Patty's coming to Thanksgiving dinner."

"We won't even be home," Sally pointed out. "We'll be at Grandma's."

The phone rang. It was Peppermint Patty again.

"Hi, Chuck," she said. "Listen, I have even greater news. Remember that kid Marcie? Her folks said it would be okay if she joined us. So you can count on two for dinner, Chuck."

Charlie Brown said, "Well, the problem is . . ."

But Peppermint Patty talked right over him. "Don't worry, Chuck. We won't make problems. We'll help clean up dishes and everything. Just save me a drumstick and the neck. See you, Chuck."

Charlie Brown hung up the phone. "How do I get myself into these things?" he wailed. "Now she's bringing Marcie, too!"

"It's your own fault for being so wishy-washy," Sally said.

And before Charlie Brown could argue, Peppermint Patty called back yet again. This time she had invited Franklin to dinner too!

"I'm doomed!" Charlie Brown exclaimed. "Three guests for Thanksgiving, and I'm not even going to be home! Peppermint Patty will hate me for the rest of my life."

But Linus had a solution. "Why not have *two* dinners? You cook the first one for your friends, then go to your grandmother's for the second one."

"But I can't cook," Charlie Brown said. "All I can make is cold cereal and toast."

Linus was sure they could do it with a little help. He told Snoopy, "Go to the garage and get a table for the backyard."

Snoopy saluted, sharp as a soldier. The world's most brilliant beagle was on the case!

As Woodstock fluttered above him Snoopy dragged a Ping-Pong table out of the overflowing garage. As soon as Snoopy opened the table, it snapped shut! He was trapped inside!

SNAP!

When the beagle broke free, so did a Ping-Pong paddle and ball. Snoopy hit the ball, then bounced over the net so fast that he returned his own serve. Snoopy played against himself until he accidentally knocked Woodstock out.

Linus walked up just in time to see the end of Snoopy's game. "We don't have time to play," Linus scolded.

Snoopy blushed. Woodstock was awake again, but seeing stars.

"We still need some chairs around the table," Linus said, directing.

Once again, Snoopy bravely battled his way through the stuffed garage.
A lawn chair proved even tougher to unfold than the Ping-Pong table!
Finally Snoopy got everything under control. He even put a tablecloth
on the Ping-Pong table.

Then it was time to start cooking. With the precision of an army, Charlie Brown, Linus, Snoopy, and Woodstock used every toaster they could to make a big stack of buttered toast. The friends popped corn and opened bags of chips, pretzels, and jelly beans.

Next Snoopy set the table. He dealt the plates like a deck of cards and expertly folded the napkins into cute little tepees.

Yikes! One of the tepees moved. Snoopy carefully lifted the napkin and found . . . Woodstock!

Ding-dong!

The doorbell rang. Peppermint Patty, Marcie, and Franklin arrived. They followed Charlie Brown to the table in the backyard.

"Say, Chuck, this looks like quite a spread," said Peppermint Patty. "I bet this is one Thanksgiving dinner we'll *never* forget!"

Snoopy carried out a big domed platter. "Aren't we going to say grace before we're served, Chuck?" Peppermint Patty asked. "It's Thanksgiving," she pointed out.

Charlie Brown wasn't sure what to do.

Linus came to the rescue. He stood up and gave a speech:

"In the year 1621, the Pilgrims had their first Thanksgiving feast. They invited the great Indian Chief Massasoit, who brought ninety of his brave Indians and a great abundance of food. Governor William Bradford and Captain Miles Standish were honored guests. Elder William Brewster, who was a minister, said a prayer that went something like this: We thank God for our homes and our food and our safety in a new land. We thank God for the opportunity to create a new world for freedom and justice!"

Peppermint Patty added, "Amen."

And with that, Snoopy lifted the lid to reveal their "feast." He shuffled the toast like cards, then plunked a piece onto a paper plate. He added a pawful of popcorn, pretzel sticks, and jelly beans. Then he threw the plate like a Frisbee across the table. *Zoom, zoom, zoom!* Plates flew to each guest.

Peppermint Patty stared in amazed disappointment. "What kind of Thanksgiving is this?!" she asked. "Don't you know anything about cooking a real Thanksgiving dinner, Chuck? Where's the turkey? Where are the mashed potatoes, cranberry sauce, and pumpkin pie? What blockhead made all this?"

Charlie Brown slunk away from the table feeling even lower than he did after losing a baseball game.

Marcie turned to Peppermint Patty. "You were kinda rough on Charles, weren't you, sir? Did he invite you to dinner, or did you invite yourself?"

"I never thought of it like that," Peppermint Patty admitted. "Do you think I hurt ol' Chuck's feelings? Golly, why can't I act right outside of a baseball game?"

Peppermint Patty convinced Marcie to apologize for her. When Marcie found Charlie Brown inside the house she said, "Don't feel bad, Charles. Peppermint Patty didn't mean all those things she said. Actually, she really likes you."

"I don't feel bad for myself," Charlie Brown explained. "I'm just sorry I ruined everyone's Thanksgiving."

"But Thanksgiving is more than eating, Charles. You heard what Linus said. The Pilgrims were thankful, and we should be thankful for just being together," Marcie said.

Peppermint Patty had been listening from the doorway. She came in and offered Charlie Brown her hand. "Apologies accepted, Chuck?" They shook hands.

Peppermint Patty continued, "There are enough problems in the world already without these silly misunderstandings." Suddenly she grinned. "Why, you're holding my hand, you sly dog."

BONG! BONG! BONG! BONG! The clock chimed. Good grief! Four o'clock already!

"We're supposed to be at Grandmother's house at four thirty," Charlie Brown said, fretting.

"I better call her and explain my dilemma." Charlie Brown picked up the phone. "Hello? Gran'ma? This is Chuck, I mean, Charlie Brown. We're going to be a little late." Then he explained about his friends still being there. "No, ma'am, they haven't eaten. As a matter of fact, they've let me know that in no uncertain terms!" Then Charlie Brown heard some wonderful news.

Marcie announced it to the rest of the gang. "We're all invited to Charlie Brown's grandmother's for Thanksgiving dinner!"

The kids all cheered!

Soon the whole gang, except for Snoopy and Woodstock, piled into the back of the station wagon.

In the car, the kids sang, "Over the river and through the woods, to grandmother's house we go! *The horse knows the way to carry the sleigh through the white and drifting snow . . . oh—*"

Charlie Brown interrupted the happy tune. "There's only one thing wrong with that."
Linus asked, "What's that, Charlie Brown?"
"My grandmother lives in a condominium."
But then he realized that it doesn't matter *where* you eat Thanksgiving dinner.
Whether it's at a condo . . .

. . . or at a doghouse, it will *always* be special when you share the feast with friends.